Monarchs at Risk

Elaine Pageler

High Noon Books

ORDER DIRECTLY FROM
ANN ARBOR PUBLISHERS LTD.
P.O. BOX 1, BELFORD
NORTHUMBERLAND NE70 7JX
TEL. 01668 214460 FAX 01668 214484
www.annarbor.co.uk

Cover Design: Jill Zwicky
Interior Illustrations: Tina Cash-Walsh

International Standard Book Number: 1-57128-004-9

0 9 8 7 6 5 4 3 2 1
3 2 1 0 9 8 7 6 5 4

You'll enjoy all the High Noon Books.
Write for a free full list of titles.

Contents

Nate and Nell's mother is an ecology professor. During the year, Dr. Kidd teaches at a college. When summer comes, people invite her to meetings all around the country. Nate and Nell often travel with her.

"Ecology is man and nature living together in harmony," their mother always says.

Nate and Nell smile. "And we're the Kidds who help," they say.

CHAPTER 1

The Return

Having an ecologist for a mother was great, thought Nate. He and Nell never knew where they would travel next. But this was a real surprise.

Their mother told them they were going to Mexico. "Maria asked me to a meeting. It's in a small village. She says it's important," she said.

"Who's Maria, Mom?" Nate asked.

"Maria was one of my students. Now she works for the Mexican Tourism office," she said.

Mom went on. "You'll miss a little school. But it's worth it to see the return," she said.

"What return?" Nell asked.

Mom grinned. "Wait and see," she said.

The Kidds flew to Mexico City. Then they took a bus to the village. It was high in the mountains. They got off the bus at the town square.

Nate could see that the village was having a festival. The park in the center was filled with people. A sign hung above them.

Both Nate and Nell were studying Spanish at school. So they could read it.

"The Day of the Dead," Nate read.

"Is that a holiday?" Nell asked.

Dr. Kidd nodded. "The second of November is the most festive of all Mexican holidays. It's to remember departed friends and family. Graves are weeded. Fresh flowers are brought to decorate them. Many families make altars in their houses. It's to welcome back the spirits of the dead."

Nate and Nell exchanged glances. Was this "the return" their mother wanted them to see?

The Kidds got their bags. Then they walked through the park. Some people sold candy skulls. Others sold flowers. There were many tables with objects on them. Families stood nearby.

"What's going on there? Are those things for sale?" Nell asked.

3

"Those are objects of their departed. The families are displaying them," her mother said.

One man sat alone on a bench. "Hi, Pedro," someone called to him.

Dr. Kidd walked over to Pedro. "I'm looking for Maria Ortega. She is staying at the inn. Will you tell me where it is?" Mom asked.

The man whittled a piece of wood. Now he stopped and pointed across the street. "I'd stay away from that woman and her wild ideas."

Just then, a shout came from the group of people. They pointed up in the air. "They're returning," they called.

Nate and Nell looked up in the sky, too. But they didn't see anything.

A young woman hurried toward them. "Dr. Kidd, I'm so glad you could come,." she said.

"Maria, this is Nate and Nell. I brought them to see the return," Dr. Kidd said.

"Do the spirits of the dead really come back today?" Nate asked.

Maria smiled. "Some of us think so. Here comes one now," she replied.

Nate looked at where she was pointing. He saw something bright orange fly through the air. It lit on a blue flower.

"That's a butterfly!" Nate exclaimed.

Nell saw the butterfly's orange wings. They had black borders and small white dots. It's a monarch," she said.

Nate looked at where she was pointing.
He saw something bright orange fly through the air.

"That's right. This part of Mexico is the winter home for monarchs. They start arriving on the Day of the Dead. So some people think spirits of the dead come on their wings," Dr. Kidd told them.

"I thought monarchs spent the winter in California," Nate said.

"So did I. We've seen them in Pacific Grove," Nell said.

"The western monarchs do. But monarchs living east of the Rocky Mountains spend their winter in Mexican forests," Mom told them.

"We hope our forests will continue to be their home. That's why we asked your mother to our meeting. We need her help," Maria said.

CHAPTER 2

A New Plan for the Village

The room was crowded that night. Dr. Kidd walked to the front. She sat at the speakers' table with Maria and the mayor.

Nate and Nell found seats and sat down. Pedro sat close by. He glared at the speakers' table.

The mayor stood up. "Thanks for coming. We called this meeting on the Day of the Dead. Maybe the spirits of our departed can help us. We need to make the right decision," he said.

A whisper went through the crowd. People nodded their heads.

The mayor went on. "Our people have been twice blessed. We live near forests that give our people work. For many years logging has put food on our tables. Also, the monarchs spend their winters in our forest. They add beauty to our lives. Most of us think the spirits of our dead return on their wings," he said.

"So what's wrong?" someone called.

The mayor clasped his hands. "We may have to choose between our two blessings," he told them.

A rumble went up from the crowd. People talked at the same time.

The mayor raised his hand for silence. "The Miguel Logging Company has two more years of work where they are now. Then they want to start cutting on Norte Mountain," he told them.

"But that's the forest the monarchs live in!" a man shouted.

"Can we tell the Miguel Logging Company no?" a woman asked.

"Yes, we can. But then they will move somewhere else. The jobs will be gone," the mayor said.

Pedro jumped up. "We need the logging company. My boss says they will mark the trees that monarchs roost on. They won't cut those down," he called.

"We have an ecologist here tonight. She knows a great deal about monarchs. Dr. Kidd, will this be enough to save our monarchs?" the mayor asked.

Mom shook her head. "No, it won't. They need the forest around their trees, too. It makes a micro-climate that shields them from the cold and wind," she said.

Pedro turned to the crowd. "Having jobs is much more important than having some monarchs around," he told them.

"The monarchs are important to us," a woman called.

"Yes, our departed return with them each year," someone else said.

"That's just an old belief. Having food on our tables is real," Pedro told them.

Once again Dr. Kidd spoke. "We have found only twelve places in Mexico where monarchs spend the winter. What will happen to the monarchs if all these villages cut their forests?" she asked.

The mayor spoke again. "Maria Ortega is here from the Mexican Tourist Office. She has an idea for us," he said.

Now Maria stood up. "I know losing your logging jobs can be scary," she began.

"That's right," Pedro called.

"Yeah," some other men said.

Maria went on. "The other villages have

the same problem. El Rosario is trying to change to tourism. They think tourists will pay to see the monarchs. This might give people in their village more money. But it means a change in their lives. Why don't you give tourism a try, too?" she asked.

"What if it doesn't work?" Pedro asked.

"You've got two years to see if it will. The bank will give a loan to fix up the old inn. Many can get jobs there. Some of you could be guides. Others could sell things," she said.

"I could make mats. They would have a monarch design," a woman called.

Others chimed in. "We could sell T-shirts, jewelry, and postcards."

13

Pedro scowled. "We don't have tourists now. Where will they come from?" he asked.

"We'll bring in a group of travel agents from the United States. Dr. Kidd has agreed to teach them about monarchs. We hope they will bring their tours here," Maria said.

Many wanted to try tourism. Pedro and some men wanted to go on logging.

At last the mayor asked for a vote. Most of the people voted for tourism.

Pedro jumped up. "That's foolish," he told them. He stomped out of the room.

Nate watched him go. Then he nudged Nell. "Look at that guy," he said.

Nell nodded. "He's trouble," she replied.

CHAPTER 3

The Breakdown

It was now February. The village had changed a great deal. The people were getting ready for tourists. Most men still worked for the logging company. But they helped at night and in their free time.

Some men were hired to remodel the inn. It wasn't done yet. But there were enough rooms for the travel agents. They would arrive today.

The Kidds came back to the village early. Having the agents come now was Mom's idea.

She wanted them to see the monarchs before they migrated north.

"We're not ready yet. But we will be when the monarchs return on the Day of the Dead," Maria said.

"How's Pedro? Is he still against your plan?" Nate asked.

"Yes, today is Sunday. So the logging company isn't working. Pedro refused to be here when the agents arrive. He left on the bus this morning. It goes to the city," Maria told them.

"When do the agents arrive?" Nell asked.

"My friend Arturo bought an older van to bring tours up to our village. He and the mayor went down to the city to get the agents. They should be here soon," she said.

Lots of people gathered in the park. They wanted to greet the agents. Maria and the Kidds walked over to the park, too. They all waited.

Maria checked her watch. "They're late. I hope nothing went wrong," she said.

Another hour went by. Finally they heard a motor. But it wasn't the van. Instead the bus stopped at the village square. Arturo, the mayor, and the travel agents got off.

Maria rushed over. "What happened?"

"The van broke down on the road. We flagged down the bus. But it was a long wait. Everyone was hot and tired," Arturo told her.

The mayor led the agents across the street. "I'm sorry about the van. But I'm sure you'll enjoy the rest of your stay. Come with me. I'll take you to your rooms," he told them.

Arturo stayed behind to talk to Maria and Dr. Kidd. "That was no accident. There was a cut in my fan belt. Someone planned for us to have a breakdown," he said.

Nell pulled at Nate's arm and pointed at the bus. "Guess who," she said.

Pedro got off. He walked over to the park bench and sat down. Then he pulled out his knife and started whittling again.

Nate frowned. "I'll bet that's the knife that cut Arturo's fan belt," he said.

CHAPTER 4

The Magic Circle

The Kidds met the travel agents after breakfast. The food had been good. They looked happier now.

"Get your jackets. We're going to see the magic circle," Dr. Kidd told them.

"What's that?" one woman asked.

"The monarchs need a special place for winter. It must be a small climate within a large one. We call this a magic circle," Dr. Kidd said.

"I still don't understand," the woman said.

Dr. Kidd went on to explain. "This place must be warm. But it must not be too warm or the monarchs would burn up their fat supply. Also, they need flowers with nectar and a water source nearby. The sun must be able to shine on them. But they must have shelter from wind and cold. The monarchs have found such a place in a forest here."

A village guide waited outside. He led the group up the mountain. Nate and Nell went along.

Last night had been cold and stormy. The clouds still covered the sun this morning. Nell buttoned her jacket around her neck. Nate did the same thing.

At last the guide stopped. He pointed to the trees. Monarchs roosted there. They hung in huge clusters and covered the branches and trunks.

"There must be millions of them. You can't see the bark or the needles," a man called.

"These butterflies are ashen-colored. I thought monarchs were orange," a woman said.

"Their wings are folded shut with the dull side out. It keeps them warmer," Mom explained.

Nate looked down at the ground. There were monarchs lying all around. "What's happened here? Why are those butterflies lying there?" he asked.

"The ones on the outside of the clusters in the trees get too cold. They fall off. This is dangerous. They may get eaten by mice," Dr. Kidd replied.

Nate picked one up. "This monarch looks all right," he said.

"Blow on it," his mother told him.

Nate cupped the monarch in his hands. Then he blew. It took several warm breaths. Then the monarch slipped out of his hands and flew to the nearest tree.

Just then the sun came out. Suddenly the trees turned bright orange. They looked as if they were on fire. The monarchs had opened their wings to catch the sunlight.

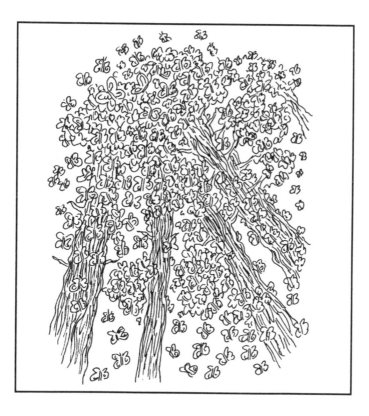

Suddenly the trees turned bright orange.
They looked as if they were on fire.

"That's beautiful!" everyone gasped.

Soon it got warmer. The monarchs started leaving their trees.

"The monarchs are going to the meadow. They will get nectar from the flowers," Dr. Kidd told everyone.

They followed and watched. The monarchs went from flower to flower. Sometimes a cloud would cover the sun. When that happened, the monarchs would hurry back to their trees.

"The monarchs need to get back while they are still warm enough to fly. If it drops below 40 degrees, they can't even crawl," Dr. Kidd told them.

"These monarchs are amazing. People will

want to see them," one agent said.

All the agents agreed. They spent most of the day watching the monarchs.

Mom met Maria when they got back. "The day went well," she said.

Her face broke out in a big smile. "I'm so glad. Thank you, Dr. Kidd," she said.

Everyone was hungry after a day in the forest. They sat down to dinner with smiles on their faces. But that changed when they started to eat. Someone had put too much salt on the food.

Nate glanced out the window. Pedro was sitting in the park. He whittled a piece of wood. There was a grin on his face.

CHAPTER 5

More About Monarchs

The next morning Dr. Kidd took the travel agents back up the mountain. It was warmer today. The monarchs had left their trees.

"Some of them may be searching for water. They get very thirsty after the long winter months. It's near the end of February now. The monarchs get more active. Soon they will mate," Mom said.

"Will the monarchs lay their eggs here?" one travel agent asked.

Mom shook her head. "The male dies after they mate. The female flies north looking for milkweed fields. That's where she will lay her eggs. Then she dies, too."

"We have monarchs in our state. The eggs turn into caterpillars. Each spins a cocoon and comes out as a butterfly," a man said.

"Yes, then those monarchs mate. That starts the cycle again. Only their life span is much shorter. Again the females fly north to lay their eggs on milkweed plants. The cycle goes on. By mid-summer the third generation gets to the south part of Canada and New England. The fourth generation comes out in late August. Then it is beginning to get colder," Mom said.

"They don't like cold," Nell said.

"That's right. So these monarchs head south. They fly back to the land of their great-great grandparents. It's about 2,000 miles away," Dr. Kidd replied.

"How do they know the way?" Nate asked.

"No one knows. Nor do they know why this generation has a much longer life span. The summer monarchs only live four or five weeks. But these live for several months. They do not mate right away. Instead they wait until the next spring. Their energy and fat are saved for the long trip south," Mom told them.

"Amazing," a man said.

"We agree," the others added.

"I have a question. Why do they only lay their eggs on milkweeds?" a man asked.

"The milkweed is poisonous to birds. The monarch caterpillars feed on the milkweed so they become poisonous, too. This keeps them safe," Dr. Kidd said.

Once again the agents were happy. There were smiles on their faces.

The mayor walked out to meet them. His face didn't have a smile. "I have bad news. There's a bad leak in a pipe. The inn has no water," he told them.

One of the travel agents shook his head. "That does it! Yes, the monarchs are amazing. But I can't bring people here. The village has too many problems," he said.

Another agent nodded his head. "The van breaks down, The food is poor. Now the inn has no water," he said.

The other agents agreed. "We're sorry because this could be a wonderful tour."

Dr. Kidd pleaded with them. "Give the village another chance. I brought you down too early. The village isn't ready yet. But they will be by this fall. Meet me in Maine on the first of November. I'll give you a tour of the monarch's migration route. We'll get back here in time to see them return."

"It sounds like fun. The village may have solved its problems by then," one agent said.

All the agents agreed to give the village one more try. Then they got on the bus and headed to the airport.

That night Nate and Nell saw Pedro sitting in the park. As usual he whittled on a stick. "I saw the agents getting on the bus. Didn't they leave early?" he asked.

"They'll be back," Nell snapped.

"You should be ashamed of yourself. All you do is complain, whittle, and cut fan belts," Nate said.

"He can put salt in food and break pipes, too," Nell added.

Pedro started to say something. But Nate and Nell didn't listen. They raced into the inn.

CHAPTER 6

The Monarch Migration

Months went by. It was the first of November. The Kidds flew to Maine and waited for the travel agents to arrive. By evening Nate and Nell had checked every name on Dr. Kidd's list.

"Everyone is here, Mom," Nate said.

Mom shook her head. "We have three more. The people from Mexico aren't here."

"Who's coming?" Nate wanted to know.

"Maria, the mayor, and Pedro," Mom replied.

"Pedro!" Nell exclaimed.

"Has he changed his mind about tourism?" Nate asked.

"No, but something has to be done about him. He could wreck the village's plan. They all need to work together. It's just like ecology and the monarch. Nothing must go wrong along their migration route. Or they won't survive," Mom said.

"So you asked Pedro to come along on this trip. Do you think it will change his mind?" Nate asked.

"I hope so. It's worth a try," Mom replied.

At last the Mexican flight arrived. Maria and the mayor rushed toward them. "Pedro didn't want to come. But we made him," they whispered.

Pedro followed. He scowled at Mom. "What's the meaning of this? I should be logging instead of flying around," he grumbled.

"We're paying you for two days. So enjoy your trip," Dr. Kidd told him.

"I'm here. Just don't expect me to have a good time," Pedro snapped.

Everyone came to the airport the next morning. Everyone seemed happy except Pedro.

Mom showed them a map of North America. "Let's go over the migration of the monarchs. They left Mexico last February and flew north in search of silkweeds. The first generation reached the Gulf states in late April or May."

"Do they lay eggs all along the route?"

someone asked.

Mom nodded. She pointed farther north on the map. "The second generation monarchs landed in states like Virginia, Missouri, Iowa, and Delaware. This was in June." she told them.

Now she pointed still higher on the map. The third generation flew north. They reached the Great Lakes, New England, and southern Canada. It's their children we'll follow today. They're the fourth generation who fly south. They weigh less than a gram. Yet they fly more than 2,000 miles," Dr. Kidd said.

"That's a long way. How can they do that?" a man asked.

"Monarchs are good gliders. They catch

rides on winds that come down from Canada. Their speeds reach 20 miles per hour. They may travel 80 miles in a day," Mom told them.

"Do they eat?" someone asked.

"Yes, they search for flowers before it gets dark each day. The monarchs left Canada in late August. They should start landing here in Maine today. The trip has taken them several weeks," Dr. Kidd said.

"How many monarchs will winter in our Mexican village?" the mayor asked.

"I don't know about your magic circle. But we've found 30 to 100 million monarchs in three acres in another place," Dr. Kidd said.

"That's a lot," the mayor said.

CHAPTER 7

Changes in the Village

Everyone liked the trip to Mexico. They all looked out the plane window. They found it hard to believe all the mountains, water, and cities the monarchs had to cross.

Arturo was waiting when they landed. He took them to the village. This time there were no problems.

The village and the inn looked good. Buildings on the square had fresh coats of paint. Monarch banners hung from their windows.

Buildings on the square had fresh coats of paint.
Monarch banners hung from their windows.

Nate was hungry. But it was still two hours until dinner. "Let's go to the bakery," he said.

The baker smiled as Nate and Nell walked in. "I hear Pedro went along on the trip. Did he enjoy it?" he asked.

"I hope so. My mother wants him to understand monarchs," Nate replied.

"Then he won't cut fan belts like he did last winter," Nell added.

The baker looked surprised. "Pedro did go to the city that day. But he didn't cut the fan belt. I know because he delivered things to the city for me. Sometimes I hire him to do that. Pedro didn't have time to go to the airport. That's where the van was parked," he said.

Nate and Nell hurried out of the bakery. "We've made a big mistake," Nate said.

Nell nodded. "Then who did it? Only Pedro, Arturo, and the mayor were in the city that day. Arturo wouldn't cut his own fan belt," she said.

"That leaves the mayor. Come on. Let's go talk to the cook at the inn," Nate told her.

The cook looked unhappy. "Don't remind me of that terrible meal. It was all my fault. The mayor brought over a letter from his sister. She is a friend. I got so interested reading it that I must have salted the food twice," she said.

Nate and Nell rushed to Dr. Kidd's room. They told her the story.

"The mayor salted the food while the cook read the letter," Nell told her.

"I bet he wrecked the water pipe, too. We should tell Pedro we're sorry," Nate said.

The Kidds found Pedro in the park. He listened as they told him how sorry they were about blaming him.

"You complained so much. So we thought you caused the problems," Nate said.

"I need to feed my family and wanted the logging company to stay. Still I wouldn't do anything like that. But you kids were right about something. All I did was whittle and complain. So I made this to prove I could do something else," he said.

He gave a sack to each of the twins.

Nate and Nell pulled out two beautifully carved monarchs. Their wings were painted orange with black borders and small white spots.

"They're beautiful!" they exclaimed.

"That's very good work," Dr. Kidd said.

"Are those for sale?" called a travel agent.

"I'll give you $25 for one of them," another travel agent said.

Pedro was surprised. "No, these belong to Nate and Nell. Give me your name and address. I'll make you one," he said.

Soon all the agents were crowding around. "Our tours will buy these, too," they said.

They wrote down their names. Then they

handed Pedro money.

After they left, Mom grinned at Pedro. "It looks like you have another job," he said.

Pedro nodded. "Maybe I'll make as much as I did logging," he said.

Nate nudged his mother. "Look, here comes the mayor," he said.

The mayor walked over with his eyes down. "I have something to confess. I am the guilty one who tried to stop tourism. It was the wrong thing to do. But I thought I was helping my village. I was afraid to try something new. The magic circle was important. But I wouldn't admit it."

"What made you change your mind?" Dr. Kidd wanted to know.

"It was the trip. I realized what we owe the rest of our world. We must save the magic circle or they won't have monarchs. Caring for them is our job," he said.

Dr. Kidd smiled at him. "I'm so glad you understand that now," she said.

A monarch flew past. Then it turned back and lit on a flower near the mayor.

"Maybe it's one of our departed. It's telling us we're doing O.K.," Pedro said.

"Perhaps it is," the mayor agreed.

"Your departed should be proud of this village. You're good ecologists," Dr. Kidd said.

"And ecology is man and nature working together," Nate and Nell chimed in.